Lenny Makes
a Wish

OXFORD
UNIVERSITY PRESS

Great Clarendon Street, Oxford OX2 6DP
Oxford University Press is a department of the University of Oxford.
It furthers the University's objective of excellence in research, scholarship,
and education by publishing worldwide. Oxford is a registered trade mark
of Oxford University Press in the UK and in certain other countries

Database right Oxford University Press (maker)

First published in 2020

British Library Cataloguing in Publication Data

Data available

ISBN: 978-01-9-275886-6

1 3 5 7 9 10 8 6 4 2

Printed in China

Paper used in the production of this book is a natural,
recyclable product made from wood grown in sustainable forests.
The manufacturing process conforms to the environmental
regulations of the country of origin.

Lenny Makes a Wish

Paula Metcalf

OXFORD
UNIVERSITY PRESS

The blossom's out, the birds are singing,
spring at last has come.
Lenny's in the meadow,
picking flowers for his mum.

He takes a rest beside a pool,
beneath a shady tree,
and spies a funny little fish
as black as black can be.

Seeing that she's all alone
makes Lenny very sad.
He very gently asks her,
'Where's your mummy or your dad?'

'I used to live quite far from here,
with all my family.
But then a storm swept us apart
and now it's only me.'

Lenny wonders what to do.
How lonely she must be!
But soon he has a great idea
and hopes that she'll agree . . .

'Do you want to be my friend?
I'm sometimes lonely too.'
The fishy nods her head and squeaks,
'I really, really do!'

So Lenny kneels beside the pool
and fishes Fishy out.
But suddenly she starts to gasp,
and flip and flap about!

'Oh no,' cries Lenny, 'I forgot!
You cannot breathe in air!'
He throws her back and, luckily,
she's none the worse for wear.

'Let's play in my pool,' Fishy says,
so Lenny jumps right in.
But straight away it's clear to him . . .

that rabbits

do not swim!

Seconds later Mum appears,
her eyes are wide with fear.
'Never play near water, Lenny!
NEVER! Do you hear?'

So Lenny says a sad goodbye,
his eyes are getting wet.
He gives the fish his scarf, and
whispers, 'So you don't forget.'

Days go by and Fishy tries
but cannot smile at all.
She cuddles Lenny's precious scarf.
And tears begin to fall.

Lenny's missing Fishy too
and often, late at night,
he looks into the endless dark
and hopes that she's all right.

But *then* there comes a night SO clear—
the stars are bright as gems!
He wishes on the biggest one,
'Please let us meet again!'

Eventually the summer comes,
the days are long and hot.
Mum and Len are having lunch,
when suddenly they spot . . .

. . . a very smiley little frog
who's hopping up the path.

They take a closer look and see
she's wearing Lenny's scarf!

'I was a *tadpole*, not a fish!'
the froggy laughs, and then
she shyly turns to Len and says,
'Do you want to be my friend?'

Lenny's happy as can be.
He can't believe it's true!
He answers with a great big grin . . .

'I really, really do!'

for my
favourite
little tadpole
∿ EMMA ∿

A note for grown-ups

Oxford Owl is a FREE and easy-to-use website packed with support and advice about everything to do with reading.

Informative videos

Hints, tips and fun activities

Top tips from top writers for reading with your child

Help with choosing picture books

For this expert advice and much, much more about how children learn to read and how to keep them reading . . .

LOOK
for Oxford Owl

www.oxfordowl.co.uk